WESTMINSTER SCHOOLS

SMYTHE GAMBRELL
LIBRARY

PRESENTED BY

Abby Couch
1986

Cate Candler

The Brothers Grimm

SNOW WHITE
and ROSE RED

Illustrated by John Wallner

Prentice-Hall, Inc., Englewood Cliffs, New Jersey

Printed in the United States of America   •J

Prentice-Hall International, Inc., London
Prentice-Hall of Australia, Pty. Ltd., Sydney
Prentice-Hall Canada, Inc., Toronto
Prentice-Hall of India Private Ltd., New Delhi
Prentice-Hall of Japan, Inc., Tokyo
Prentice-Hall of Southeast Asia Pte. Ltd., Singapore
Whitehall Books Limited, Wellington, New Zealand
Editora Prentice-Hall do Brasil LTDA., Rio de Janeiro

10 9 8 7 6 5 4 3 2 1

Library of Congress Cataloging in Publication Data

Grimm, Jacob, 1785-1863.
  Snow White and Rose Red.

  Translation of: Schneeweisschen und Rosenroth.
  Summary: A bear, befriended by two sisters during the
winter, returns one day to reward them royally for their
kindness.
  [1. Fairy tales. 2. Folklore—Germany] I. Grimm,
Wilhelm, 1786-1859. II. Wallner, John C., ill.
III. Title
PZ8.G882Sn   1984   398.2'2'0943   [E]   84-4910
ISBN 0-13-815234-9

For Rachel Elizabeth

A poor widow once lived in a little cottage with a garden in front of it. In the garden grew two rose trees, one bearing white roses and the other red. The widow had two children who were just like the two rose trees; one was called Snow White and the other Rose Red. They were the sweetest and best children in the world, but Snow White was quieter and more gentle than Rose Red. Rose Red loved to run about the fields and meadows and to pick flowers and catch butterflies; but Snow White sat at home with her mother and helped her in the house, or read aloud to her when there was no work to do.

The two children loved each other so dearly that they always walked hand in hand whenever they went out together. And when Snow White said, "We will never desert each other," Rose Red answered, "No, not as long as we live"; and the mother added, "Whatever one gets she shall share with the other."

The sisters often roamed about in the woods gathering berries, and animals came up to them in the most confiding manner. The little hare would eat a cabbage leaf from their hands, the deer grazed beside them, the stag would bound past them merrily, and the birds remained on the branches and sang to them. No harm ever befell them. If they tarried late in the wood and night overtook them, they lay down together on the moss and slept till morning, and their mother knew they were quite safe and never felt anxious about them.

Snow White and Rose Red kept their mother's cottage so beautifully clean and neat that it was a pleasure to go into it. In summer Rose Red looked after the house, and every morning before her mother awoke she placed a bunch of flowers beside the bed, and a rose from each tree.

In winter Snow White lit the fire and put on the kettle, which was made of brass, so beautifully polished that it shone like gold.

In the evening when the snowflakes fell, their mother said, "Snow White, go and close the shutters." Then they sat around the fire, while the mother put on her spectacles and read aloud from a big book, and the two girls listened and sat and spun. Beside them on the floor lay a little lamb, and behind them perched a little white dove with its head tucked under its wing.

One evening as they sat thus cozily together someone knocked at the door. The mother said, "Rose Red, open the door quickly! It must be some traveler seeking shelter."

Rose Red hastened to unbar the door, and thought she saw a poor man standing outside. But it was no such thing! It was a bear who poked his thick black head through the door.

Rose Red screamed aloud and sprang back in terror. The lamb began to bleat, the dove flapped its wings, and Snow White ran and hid behind her mother's bed. But the bear said, "Don't be afraid; I won't hurt you. I am half frozen, and only wish to warm myself a little."

"My poor bear," said the mother, "lie down by the fire, only take care you don't burn your fur." Then she called out, "Snow White and Rose Red, come out. The bear will do you no harm. He is a good honest creature."

So they both came out of their hiding places, and gradually the lamb and dove drew near too, and they all forgot their fear. The bear asked the children to beat the snow out of his fur, and they fetched a brush and scrubbed him until he was dry. Then the beast stretched himself in front of the fire and growled quite happily and comfortably.

The children soon grew quite at their ease with him. They tugged his fur with their hands, put their small feet on his back and rolled him about here and there, or took a hazel wand and beat him with it; and if he growled they only laughed. The bear submitted to everything with the best possible good nature. Only when they went too far he cried, "O children, spare my life!"

When it came time to retire for the night and the children went to bed, the mother said to the bear, "You can lie there on the hearth. It will be shelter for you from the cold and wet." As soon as day dawned the children let him out, and he trotted over the snow into the wood.

From this time the bear came every evening at the
same hour, and lay down by the hearth and let the
children play what pranks they liked with him. They grew
so accustomed to him that the door was never shut till
their friend had made his appearance.

When spring came and all outside was green, the bear
said one morning to Snow White, "Now I must go away
and not return again for the whole summer."

"Where are you going, dear bear?" asked Snow White.

"I must go into the wood and protect my treasure from the wicked dwarfs. In winter, when the earth is frozen hard, they are obliged to remain underground, for they can't work their way through. But now, when the sun has thawed and warmed the ground, they break through and come up to spy the land and steal what they can. What once falls into their hands and into their caves is not easily brought back to light."

    Snow White was quite sad over their friend's departure.
She unbarred the door for him and the bear, stepping
out, caught a piece of his fur in the door knocker. Snow
White thought she caught sight of glittering gold
beneath it, but she couldn't be certain of it; and the bear
ran hastily away and soon disappeared behind the trees.

A short time after this the mother sent the children into the forest to collect firewood. In their wanderings they came upon a big tree that lay felled on the ground. On the trunk among the long grass they noticed something jumping up and down, but what it was they couldn't tell.

When they approached nearer they saw it was a dwarf with a wizened face and a beard a yard long. The end of the beard was jammed into a cleft of the tree, and the little man sprang about like a dog on a chain, and didn't seem to know what to do.

He glared at the girls with his fiery little eyes and screamed out, "What are you standing there for? Can't you come and help me?"

"What were you doing, little man?" asked Rose Red.

"You stupid, inquisitive goose!" replied the dwarf. "I wanted to split the tree in order to get little chips of wood for our kitchen fire. I had driven in the wedge and all was going well, but the horrid wood was so slippery that it suddenly sprang out, and the tree closed up so suddenly that I had no time to take my beautiful white beard out. So here I am stuck fast and I can't get away; and you silly, smooth-faced, milk-and-water girls just stand and laugh. Ugh, what wretches you are!"

The children did all in their power, but they couldn't get the beard out; it was wedged in far too firmly. "I will run and fetch somebody," said Rose Red.

"Crazy blockheads!" snapped the dwarf. "What's the good of calling anyone else? You're already two too many for me. Does nothing better occur to you than that?"

"Don't be so impatient," said Snow White. "I'll help." And taking her scissors out of her pocket, she cut the end off his beard.

As soon as the dwarf felt himself free, he seized a bagful of gold which was hidden among the roots of the tree, lifted it up, and muttered aloud, "Curse these rude wretches, cutting off a piece of my splendid beard!" Then he swung the bag over his back and disappeared without so much as looking at the children again.

Shortly after this Snow White and Rose Red went out to get some fish. As they approached the stream they saw something which looked like an enormous grasshopper springing toward the water as if it were going to jump in. They ran forward and recognized the dwarf.

"Where are you going?" asked Rose Red. "You're surely not going to jump into the water!"

"I'm not such a fool!" screamed the dwarf. "Don't you see that horrid fish is trying to drag me in?" The little man had been sitting on the bank fishing, when unfortunately the wind had entangled his beard in the line. Immediately afterwards a big fish bit, and the feeble little creature had no strength to pull it out. The fish had the upper fin and dragged the dwarf toward him. The dwarf clung with all his might to every rush and blade of grass, but it didn't help him much. He had to follow every movement of the fish and was in great danger of being drawn into the water.

The girls came up just at the right moment, held him firm, and did all they could to disentangle his beard from the line; but in vain—beard and line were in a hopeless muddle. Nothing remained but to produce the scissors and cut the beard again.

When the dwarf perceived what they were about, he yelled to them, "Do you call that manners, you toadstools! to disfigure a fellow's face? It wasn't enough that you shortened my beard before, but you must now cut off the best of it. I can't appear like this before my own people. I wish you'd stayed at home where you belong." Then he fetched a sack of pearls that lay among the rushes, and without saying another word he dragged it away and soon disappeared behind a stone.

It happened soon after this the mother sent the two
girls to town to buy needles, thread, laces, and ribbons.
Their road led over a heath where huge boulders lay
scattered here and there. While trudging along they saw
a big bird hovering in the air, circling slowly above them,
but always descending lower, till at last it settled on a
rock not far from them. Immediately afterwards they
heard a sharp, piercing cry. They ran forward and saw
with horror that the eagle had pounced on their old
friend the dwarf and was about to carry him off.

The tender-hearted children seized hold of the little man, and struggled so long with the bird that at last he let go his prey. When the dwarf had recovered from the first shock he screamed in his squeaking voice, "Couldn't you have treated me more carefully? You have torn my thin little coat all to shreds, useless, awkward creatures that you are!" Then he took a bag of precious stones and vanished under the rocks into his cave. The girls were accustomed to his ingratitude, and went on their way and did their business in town.

On their way home, as they were again crossing the heath, they surprised the dwarf pouring out his precious stones on an open space, for he had thought no one would pass by at so late an hour. The evening sun shone on the glittering stones, and they gleamed so beautifully that the children stood still and gazed at them.

"What are you standing there gaping for?" screamed the dwarf, and his ashen-gray face became scarlet with rage. He was about to depart with these angry words when a sudden growl was heard and a black bear trotted out of the wood.

The dwarf jumped up in a great fright, but he hadn't time to reach his place of retreat, for the bear was already close to him. Then he cried in terror, "Dear Mr. Bear, spare me! I'll give you all my treasure. Look at these beautiful precious stones lying there. Spare my life! What pleasure would you get from a poor, feeble little fellow like me? You won't feel me between your teeth. There, lay hold of these two girls—they will be a tender morsel for you, as fat as young quails; eat them up instead." But the bear, paying no attention to his words, gave the evil little creature one blow with his paw and he never moved again.

The girls had run away, but the bear called after them, "Snow White and Rose Red, don't be afraid. Wait, and I'll come with you." Then they recognized his voice and stood still, and when the bear was quite close to them his skin suddenly fell off, and a handsome man stood beside them, all dressed in gold.

"I am a king's son," he said, "and have been doomed by that wicked dwarf, who had stolen my treasure, to roam about the woods as a wild bear till his death should set me free. Now he has received his well-merited punishment."

    Snow White married him and Rose Red married his brother, and they divided between them the great treasure the dwarf had collected in his cave. The old mother lived for many years peacefully with her children. She took the two rose trees from her garden with her, and they stood in front of her window, and every year they bore the finest red and white roses.